Ralph is the only boy in his whole family.

He lives at home with his mum, gran and three sisters.

Even their cat is a girl.

His oldest sister, Kia, is super bossy and shouts "RAAAAAAAAALPH!" so loud that the house rattles.

His twin sister, Petra, is really clever. She always likes to test Ralph by asking him really difficult questions.

His younger sister, Rose, likes to play all of her games with Ralph. She's not too annoying really, just a bit... PINK.

After school on Monday, Ralph went shopping with Mum. She always gave him the shopping list to tick off as they went around the store.

When he saw the giant bag of cat food, he stood tall and said, "Don't worry Mum. I'm SO STRONG!"

He lifted the bag with all his muscles and placed it into the trolley.

Ralph hoped everyone down the pet aisle saw his super strength too!

On Tuesday, they went to the dentist. Ralph offered to go first to show his sisters how brave he was. Ralph took a deep breath and slowly climbed into the chair. He was nervous but it was over quickly.

Bertie says:

Brush your teeth for 2 minutes!

Certificate

I'm a SUPER brusher!

After his check up, Ralph chose a sticker. "It's a superhero, like me!"

On Wednesday, Mum made Ralph, Kia and Rose go to watch Petra's chess tournament.

After what felt like FOREVER, the man with a microphone stood up and announced the winner.

"Peggy!"

Petra looked so sad and Ralph felt so helpless.

At home, Ralph curled up on Gran's lap. He still felt disappointed for poor Petra and Gran always made him feel better.

Gran handed Ralph a dusty old box and told him that his Grandpa was a real life superhero!

Ralph's eyes widened with excitement!

Ralph pulled out an old, tatty newspaper, a medal and a letter.

"Where is the cape?" Ralph asked, confused. Gran laughed. "Not all superheroes wear capes!"

Ralph listened carefully as Gran read the letter out loud to him.

"Dear Leo, Thank you for your hard work in the village. Every weekend you keep the streets tidy by litter picking. You are our hero!"

Ralph couldn't help but feel a little disappointed.

He thought Grandpa had rescued a puppy from a fire, or lifted a car, or flew to space!

He couldn't understand how picking up litter made Grandpa a hero.

Maybe that's all superheroes could do back in the old days?

At break on Thursday, Ralph was fighting off the villains when he noticed a little boy sitting alone on the playground bench, he looked sad. Ralph wandered over to him, feeling a bit shy. "Are you ok?" he asked. The boy sniffed. "I'm new. I don't know anybody yet".

Ralph sat down next to him.

They talked and asked each other lots of questions.

Ralph discovered that Henry had two Dads, liked playing with lego and baking cakes. Ralph told Henry that he wanted to be a superhero one day, Henry wanted to be a chef, a florist and a builder.

They must have been talking for a long time because the end of break bell rang and all the other children had already gone to their classrooms!

Ralph and Henry spent the rest of the day sitting together. He saw how sad Henry was on the bench and how happy he seemed to be now.

Ralph introduced Henry to all of his friends and they ate snacks at the table.

He liked this feeling.

On Friday they had assembly, and Ralph saved Henry a space in the hall.

Our values
- Be kind
- Be helpful
- Have respect
- Try your best

"We have a VERY important person in the room" said the Headteacher.

"This person is so special. They are strong, fearless, brave and helpful. This child is a true Superhero".

The headteacher explained that she had found a note in the school office with a paper medal.

She read it aloud.

Thank you!

To my new friend, Ralph. Thank you for talking to me yesterday when I had no one to play with. You said you wanted to be a Superhero one day, but I think you already are one.

The headteacher called Ralph up on stage and his heart started beating so fast, all he could hear was the 'boom boom boom' in his chest.

Ralph smiled nervously as he watched all the children and teachers cheering and clapping for him. He felt a rush of love in his heart as he looked at Henry and smiled. Henry looked super proud of his friend.

Ralph had the best day ever. Everyone at school thought he was brilliant and the teachers kept telling him how the world needs more heroes like Ralph in it. He felt on top of the world! He ran home after school to tell his Gran about his day.

"I always knew you were a superhero" she said, as she snuggled him tightly.

"Not all heroes wear capes, remember!"

Now Ralph knew how Grandpa must have felt when he got his medal.

Printed in Great Britain
by Amazon

81598298R00016